Just
Three

Just Three

Lorna Schultz Nicholson

ORCA BOOK PUBLISHERS

Library and Archives Canada Cataloguing in Publication

Title: Just three / Lorna Schultz Nicholson.
Names: Schultz Nicholson, Lorna, author.
Series: Orca currents.

Description: Series statement: Orca currents

Identifiers: Canadiana (print) 20190065885 |
Canadiana (ebook) 20190065915 | ISBN 9781459821699 (softcover) |
ISBN 9781459821705 (PDF) | ISBN 9781459821712 (EPUB)

Classification: LCC PS8637.C58 J87 2019 | DDC jc813/.6—dc23

Library of Congress Control Number: 2019934036
Simultaneously published in Canada and the United States in 2019

Summary: In this high-interest novel for middle readers, thirteen-year-old
twins Rory and Jillian try to get their father to consider dating.

*Orca Book Publishers is committed to reducing the consumption
of nonrenewable resources in the making of our books. We make
every effort to use materials that support a sustainable future.*

Orca Book Publishers gratefully acknowledges the support for its publishing
programs provided by the following agencies: the Government of Canada,
the Canada Council for the Arts and the Province of British Columbia
through the BC Arts Council and the Book Publishing Tax Credit.

Edited by Tanya Trafford
Cover artwork by Shutterstock.com/Master1305 and iStock.com/MissTuni
Author photo by Focus Sisters Photography

ORCA BOOK PUBLISHERS
orcabook.com

Printed and bound in Canada.

22   21   20   19   •   4   3   2   1

To Steph and Jenn at YABS.
Thanks for all you do!

Chapter One

The white part of my poached eggs wobbled. Like Jell-O that hadn't set properly. They looked so disgusting, my stomach wobbled too. I wanted to throw up.

"These eggs aren't cooked," Rory whispered. "Look, Jillian," he said, holding up his fork and letting the gooey egg drip down onto his plate. "White snot."

"Ewwww. You're so gross." He might be my twin brother, but we are nothing alike.

"I don't think she's ever made poached eggs before," Rory continued, still whispering. "She must have looked up how to cook them on the internet but forgot to read all the steps. She should stick to fried."

"Yeah, I guess," I said. I did feel a little bad. In a way, this attempt at cooking our eggs differently was my fault. I'd told Rebecca, our housekeeper, that fried eggs were not very healthy, especially when she cooked them with soooo much butter.

Rory laughed as he scooped his fork under the other lump on his plate. A big brown lump. It looked like dog food. "And what is *this*?"

"Corned-beef something or other," I said. I didn't bother to whisper. "It's seriously from a *can*."

Rebecca didn't hear me. She was over by the sink, singing some song about sunshine. I glanced over at my father. He was gobbling his breakfast down. Really? Mom had never made us anything that looked like this. She'd made things like French toast with cinnamon, waffles with homemade jam, and scrambled eggs that were cooked properly and had real cheese grated on top. None of this fake stuff.

"I'm not eating this." I got up and took my plate to the trash. I scraped the lumps into the bin and put my plate in the dishwasher. Rebecca didn't even notice. I grabbed a bagel from the bread basket. That's when Rebecca turned.

"You're hungry this morning," she said.

"Um, sort of," I replied.

"Maybe I should pack you two sandwiches then," she said, smiling.

"I can make my own lunch." I wasn't a baby. Plus her lunches sucked.

"No, no, honey. That's what I'm here for," Rebecca said, still smiling. She has, like, this huge smile where all her teeth show.

I had to smile back because, well, I just did. Rebecca has this way of making everyone smile. Teachers, grocery-store clerks, even my friends. Even though she really annoys me, that smile is hard to resist.

Rebecca started working at our house before my mother passed away two years ago. My mother actually hired her. She felt we needed someone "nice" and "friendly" to help us out. Maybe we did then. But now that we are thirteen I don't see the point of her still coming around.

In the beginning, Rebecca had done housework, like vacuuming and dusting, the hard stuff Mom had struggled with. But when my mom got too sick to even get upstairs, Rebecca had helped take care of her. There was a hospital bed set up in the middle of the dining room, and Rebecca made sure my mom had everything she needed, even changing her clothes, while my dad went to work. He is a biology professor at the university, and my mom insisted he "get to class." She also insisted that Rory and I focus on our schoolwork and not fuss over her either. I had offered to stay home from school to help, but Mom said no. That's just who she was. We were always first.

I looked over at Rory, who had drowned the corned-beef whatever in ketchup and was pushing it around and around his plate. Both Rory and my dad had their heads down. Brown hair flopped over their eyes, glasses slipped down their noses. Both out of tune with the real world. It was like they were the twins, not Rory and me.

My dad must have felt me staring because he looked up and gave me his lopsided grin. Then he pushed up his glasses, wiped his mouth with his napkin and stood up. Patting his stomach, he said, "That was delicious, Rebecca."

"Glad to hear." She almost sang her words.

Rory looked at me and grinned. Under the table, our rescue dog, Curly (Mom had named her as soon as she spotted her at the shelter), was licking Rory's plate. When Rory stood to take his plate to the dishwasher, there wasn't a scrap left on it. "I cleaned my plate," he whispered as he walked past me.

"I used to eat Spam as a kid," said my dad. He was obviously talking to

Rebecca, because what the heck was Spam? "My grandmother fed it to us."

"Me too!" said Rebecca, giggling. She held up her hand and my dad gave her a high five. No joke. A high five. In our kitchen. Rebecca had to jump a bit to reach his hand (she is pretty short), and her mop of frizzy hair bobbed up and down. Months ago I offered to show her how to use my flat iron, but she refused. She prefers the "au naturel" look.

Rebecca started wiping off the counter with a wet rag, putting her entire body into the movement. She might be little, but she is very muscular. This past year I have grown taller than her. But where my arms are like twigs, hers are like bricks.

Dad and Rebecca went on and on about that lousy breakfast and the good ol' days. Had they totally missed that Rory and I had barely touched it?

Now my father was laughing so hard he had to hold his stomach. Rebecca too. She sounded like a donkey braying. Then she snorted. Snorted!

I left the kitchen in a huff. I had to get ready for work. Rory followed me. We both have summer volunteer positions at a kids' camp at the local community center. We are in charge of the arts-and-crafts part.

"They laugh at the stupidest things," I said, climbing the stairs to my room.

"It's just olden-days talk," said Rory.

"Rebecca has no class," I said. "Did you hear her snort?"

Rory shrugged. "She's okay."

"Not around Dad she's not." I yanked open the door to my bedroom.

"Well, I think she's nice," said Rory. "Mom thought so too."

Why did he have to bring that up? I deflated like a balloon. Mom *did* like Rebecca, that was true. And I had to admit, Rory is right. She is nice. But she sure isn't good at her job. And she has my dad completely fooled.

I closed my door. As I brushed my hair, I stared at the photo of my mother I had stuck in the corner of the mirror. Dressed in cool jeans and a white sweater, she was posing for the camera. My dad always said she was the most beautiful woman in the world. Her black hair fell down her back, and her dark eyes shone. I think that might have been the worst for her—when she lost all her thick, shiny hair. My mother was half South Asian, which makes me a quarter. But I didn't get her dark hair or eyes. Neither did Rory.

I touched the photo. "I get it, Mom," I whispered to the photo. "We did need Rebecca. But I'm thirteen now. And I think Dad likes her too much. I'm sure *that* wasn't in your plan."

I pulled my brown hair into a ponytail, grabbed my backpack and went to the washroom to brush my teeth. And apply a tiny bit of mascara. Oh, and lip gloss too.

I was ready before anyone else, so I headed outside into the bright sun. I leaned against the car and scrolled on my phone. As soon as I heard the front door open, I called out, "Shotgun!"

"No fair!" said Rory. "You got it yesterday."

"And the day before and the day before," I said, swinging open the car door.

Yes, I got in the front seat. I had something I needed to talk to Dad about. I waited for him to back out of our driveway first though. Last time I'd distracted him while backing out, he'd hit the trash can. As soon as we were on the road, I took a deep breath.

"Dad," I said.

"Uh-huh." He was leaning back in his seat now, one hand on the wheel and one arm out his open window. We were driving maybe two miles an hour. Well, not quite, but close.

"Why do we keep Rebecca on?" I paused, but only for a second. "Rory and I can take care of ourselves now."

"That's true," said my father.

"I like her," said Rory. I turned and gave him a look.

"And just for the record," I continued, "I'm a *way* better cook."

"True again. You did inherit your mother's culinary skills."

"So, why then?"

"She's like family," my dad said, reaching to turn on the radio.

Like family? What the heck did *that* mean?

Chapter Two

"We have to do something," I said to Rory as soon as we were out of the car.

"What do you mean? Everything is planned for us," he said. "Today it's *Let's make a mask day*." He used his fingers for quotation marks.

"Not about camp," I snapped. "About *Dad*. And Rebecca."

Rory pushed up his glasses and squinted at me. He had a completely brainless look on his face. I started to explain what I meant, but just then Trevor, another camp volunteer, hip-checked Rory. He started howling in laughter as Rory lurched forward.

Then Trevor turned to me and said, "Hiiii, Jill-i-an." He went to hip-check me too, but I moved out of the way. So instead, Trevor grabbed Rory and put him in a headlock. Rory squirmed and got away, then turned and rammed into him headfirst. They both laughed as they wrestled like bear cubs. I'm sorry, but I had to roll my eyes.

"You guys are acting like you're five," I said. "Like the kids at camp."

Trevor stopped for a moment and pushed his black, curly bangs off his face. Sweat was beading on his forehead. "Come on, Jill-i-an, lighten up a little," he said as he tried to bump shoulders with me.

"Whatever," I said, moving out of range again. "I've got a lot on my mind today."

"We're making masks!" Rory shook his head at me. "It's not rocket science."

"My thoughts don't have anything to do with making masks."

Trevor glanced at his watch. "I have to run," he said. "Soccer today. See you at lunch." He was considered the jock at the camp and worked with the sports kids. Rory watched him take off, like a little puppy dog that was being left behind.

"You're obsessed with Trevor," I said.

He shrugged. "He's cool."

All the girls at school did have the hots for Trevor. He was a sports star at school too. Personally, I didn't see what the big deal was. Sure, he was cute and super athletic, but he was also kind of annoying.

Rory and I walked into our arts-and-crafts room. Suddenly we were surrounded by color. The room made my heart skip. As soon as the kids spotted us, they came running over. One little girl, Abigail, wrapped her arms around my legs. "You're here!" she exclaimed.

"Of course I am," I said, smiling down at her.

She looked up at me with her big eyes. "I'm putting glitter on my mask," she told me. She held her arms out wide. "This much glitter."

I laughed. "Okay." Then I held up my hand, and she gave me a high five. (Summer camp is where high fives should take place.) I shook my head, remembering Dad and Rebecca in the kitchen that morning.

The arts-and-crafts room had long work tables that were covered in plastic tablecloths and mapped with random paint streaks. Stacked bins, crammed with scissors, rulers, glue sticks, pipe cleaners, cotton balls, construction paper, buttons, colored pencils and glitter jars, lined the walls. Other bins, filled with scraps of material and random stuff, sat on the floor. It was like craft materials oozed out of the walls.

Our head instructor, Belinda (the one who actually got paid), gave Rory and me our morning instructions. Then she told the kids what they were going to be doing. Basically, our job was to help those little fingers draw, cut and stick whatever they wanted to make their masks. Some created animals, others made superheroes, and there were more than a few magical creatures (including messy, sparkly fairy dust). Abigail made a witch's mask. She told me the witch was good *and* evil.

"She looks mean," she said, pointing to the black coloring she'd done. "But she's not. She's nice." Now she pointed to the pink glitter all around the edges. "This is who she really is inside. She can't help it if she's not pretty."

"You did a good job," I said. "Now how about you put your mask down so it can dry?" I stood up and stretched, glancing at the clock. "Now we're going to go play outside for a bit." Eleven thirty already. Time had flown by.

"Good job, Winston," I heard Rory say to a little boy whose mask was a dog with a huge tongue made out of pink felt. Winston started barking, and Rory laughed. Okay, now it was really time to go outside.

The morning session always ended with outside playtime. It was mostly just a lot of running around and screaming. And soon it turned to crying. Because they were five and tired and hungry.

My stomach growled too. Once the parents had picked up their kids, we got an hour for lunch before the second group showed up. We usually met up with all the other volunteers outside at the picnic table. We all went to the same school.

I was the last one to get to the table. The only spot available was at the end, beside Trevor. On his other side sat Charlotte, a girl who moved here from Kenya a few years back. She is really nice. Like Trevor, she is a great athlete. She works in the sport camp with him. Rory sat on the other side of the table, wedged between Victor and Samantha. They work in the computer camp.

Rory had lifted the top piece of bread off his sandwich. He was staring, just staring. Plunking myself down, I yanked out my sandwich. What had she made *this* time? If Rory was struggling, I was in deep trouble.

I opened the bread and stared down at some weird meat, slices of cucumber and jam. Not mustard. Not ketchup. *Jam.*

"I can't eat this." I slapped the sandwich back together.

Trevor started howling. "What *was* that?"

I glared at him. "I didn't make it. I told our housekeeper I could make my own lunch," I said. "But, no, she insisted."

Victor held out half of an amazing-looking sub. "Here. I can't eat all of mine," he said.

I quickly glanced at him. I knew the polite thing would be to say, *No, it's okay—it's your sandwich*, but I was starving. Turkey and lettuce and cheese on a super-fresh bun. "Thanks," I said instead. "That's so nice of you!"

Then Trevor passed one of his wraps over to Rory. "Here, dude, have some of my chicken wrap. I made it this morning."

"Great! Thanks!" Rory snatched the wrap in a heartbeat.

Silence took over for a few seconds while we all wolfed down our food. Then Trevor said, "You should make your own sandwiches. I started making mine when I was ten because my dad had no clue. One of my dad's *girlfriends*"—he used quotation marks for the word *girlfriend*—"made us this picnic once with nasty cardboard vegan sandwiches. Then my dad started making them for our lunches. Even after they broke up! She was the worst match he had."

"What do you mean by *match*?" Victor asked.

I glanced at Victor again, and my lip curled up into a tiny smile. He was so curious, always asking questions in this serious way. He was kind of cute too.

"A *match*"—again Trevor used quotation marks—"means he met her on this dating site called, and wait until you hear the name, *organiclove.com*."

Samantha laughed. "That's really what it's called?"

"Yeah. And it's for old people, like forty. My dad has been on a lot of dates. And I tell you, he's met some real winners." He tilted his head. "Not all of them have been disasters though."

Something sparked inside me. An idea. "So your dad just signed up?" I asked slowly.

"Yeah. Well, I helped him create his profile, and then they do the rest. They match you up with people they think will be a good fit. You know, like *organic*. So lame."

I looked hard at Trevor. Like, stared him right in the eyes. "So does it work? It sounds like your dad hasn't found love yet."

"Well…" He made a face. "My dad might be part of the problem," he said. "I mean, my mom's pretty awesome, and they didn't work out."

I glanced at Rory to see if he was getting why I was asking so many questions. But he was busy eating his wrap.

I tapped the table. Thinking. Thinking. My idea was getting bigger.

Chapter Three

Dad drives us to the community center in the mornings, but after work we walk home. Today the sun shone in a perfect blue sky, and I inhaled the smell of summer. Freshly cut grass. Flowers. Heat coming off the pavement. I was so glad I'd worn shorts today. Rory walked beside me, his flip-flops making slapping noises. He was also talking nonstop about, who else, Trevor.

"Did you see him play with that soccer ball? He kicked it up and hit it with his head, then kicked it with his heel. Behind him!"

"I'm more interested in what he said about his dad and his dates."

"What?" Rory pretended to kick a soccer ball. Rory was A+ smart but not so athletic. His flip-flop went sailing through the air.

"That dating site Trevor mentioned." I caught Rory's sandal and gave it back to him.

"Ouch," said Rory. He stopped to pick a stone out of his foot before slipping the flip-flop back on.

"Didn't you hear him talking about his dad?"

We started walking again. "I might have been too interested in the wrap he gave me," said Rory. "Man, was it good.

It had *bacon* in it. I'm making my own lunch tomorrow, and I'm putting some bacon in my sandwich."

"Me too," I said. "Making my lunch, that is. I'll pass on the bacon. But I need you to listen to me for a second, Rory. You do remember it's Dad's birthday tomorrow?"

"Yeah. And I even know what I'm going to say in my card."

Our dad only ever wants a written note in a card for his birthday. Usually we get him a gift too though. Something small. He always says he likes the cards the best and tells us we don't need to buy him anything. Says it every year.

"You got him that Hawaiian shirt," I said. It was a super ugly, flowered, old-man kind of shirt, but Rory thought Dad would love it. He was probably right.

"It can be from both of us," he said.

"I might give him another gift."

"We don't need another gift. The shirt is great."

"Rory, you need to listen to me. I know Rebecca tries, and Mom wanted her to take care of us, but I don't think she's working anymore. I think Dad needs to go on a date. Maybe even get a girlfriend. It might be time for Rebecca to move on, find a family with younger kids. Like we were when she started with us. She is really good at playing games and stuff."

"Dad? On a date?" Rory burst out laughing. "I don't think that's such a good idea."

"Rory, I'm serious. I think we should set him up on that dating site. You know, the one Trevor talked about. *Organic Love.*"

"I don't think that's a very good gift."

"Well I do."

"Well I don't."

"I. Do." Rory was stubborn, like Dad. I had to try something else. "You got him the shirt, so I want to give him something too. It's only fair. But I think both gifts should come from both of us."

"Then go buy him some shorts to go with the shirt."

"No! I want to set him up on that *organiclove.com* site. And you're going to help me."

"No. I'm. Not."

"Whatever," I said. "It's going to work. You'll see."

"I'm still not helping."

We didn't speak for the rest of the walk home. I knew Rory was mad at me because that's the only time he doesn't talk. He stayed in the backyard to kick his soccer ball around. I went inside. As I entered the house, I heard Rebecca singing. Curly came bounding out from the family room, wagging her tail at full force. I bent over and picked her up.

Rebecca must have heard the door because she stopped singing and came out from the kitchen. She had flour in her hair.

"Are you baking?" I asked. *Please don't tell me she's making my dad a cake.*

"I'm trying to make something special for your dad for his birthday."

Great. "Good luck with that," I said, trying to smile. "That reminds me, I have to go upstairs and write his card."

"It's so wonderful that you kids write those cards for him every year. He's a lucky man."

"Um, thanks," I said, softening a little. She does have such a kind side.

Then she laughed. "Maybe not so lucky with my cake though. I don't think it turned out."

Why didn't that surprise me?

With Curly still in my arms, I took the stairs two at a time. When I got to my bedroom, I saw the laundry on my bed. Not folded, just dumped. It was my red load. Our school colors are red, so I have a lot of red T-shirts and sweats. I play on the badminton and volleyball teams. I had actually told Rebecca I would do my own laundry after she ruined my favorite silk shirt by putting it in the dryer.

I noticed Rory's Toronto Raptors shirt poking out of the pile. I yanked the white shirt out of my pile of red. I mean, I yanked his used-to be-white shirt out. It was now *pink*.

I looked at Curly. "Rory is going to be so mad," I said to her. She jumped on my bed and curled into a ball. I realized I could use this to convince Rory to go along with my plan.

I took the shirt to Rory's room across the hall. I folded it nicely and put it on his bed. Then I went back to my room and sat on my bed beside Curly to fold my own laundry.

As I folded, I remembered being little and helping my mom do exactly the same thing. We would sing. It was a game she would play with me, and I got to choose the song. When I was little, the songs were silly kid songs from anything Disney. When I got a little older, we sang Taylor Swift songs. Sometimes we ended up dancing.

I stopped folding and closed my eyes. "Why me?" Curly just looked at me.

I petted her gently. She sighed and closed her eyes. Mom had brought Curly home for us. She'd thought she was adorable and needed love. Curly had been her dog before Mom died, and now she was kind of mine. Why was it me who had a mother who died? My heart just throbbed. Ached so bad I could hardly breathe. It felt like a heavy weight was pressing against my heart with every ache. My eyes stung. The tears began to trickle down my cheeks. Life without Mom was so complicated.

I sat there for a few seconds. Then I wiped my tears and finished folding. She wasn't coming back, and there was nothing I could do. I put all my clothes away.

I picked up my laptop from my nightstand. Sitting on my bed, I logged in. I pulled up the website Trevor had mentioned. I was reading through the home page when I heard Rory coming up the stairs. I waited. Then I heard him yell. And his footsteps coming toward my room.

"Come in," I said sweetly. Time to get to the future.

He flung open the door. "My Raptors shirt!"

"Awwww. That sucks," I said.

"This was my absolute most favorite shirt! Now it's ruined. She's getting worse! Those sandwiches today were so gross." Rory didn't lose his cool often, but it was something to see.

I nodded. "She's distracted."

"Distracted?" he asked.

Rory was so clueless. "She's in love," I said.

He frowned. "With who?"

"Dad."

"*Dad?*"

"You haven't noticed?"

"Not really. They're just friends, aren't they?"

I sat up and turned my laptop toward him. "We need to set Dad up on this. Find him a girlfriend. Someone more like him. More like Mom. *She* never wrecked the laundry."

"O-kay," said Rory.

He sounded a bit sad.

Chapter Four

The next morning I woke up early and tiptoed downstairs so I wouldn't wake anyone. A birthday card was propped up on the kitchen table. I knew it was from Rebecca. She had the day off but must have left it here last night. I couldn't help myself. I picked it up and flipped it over. The envelope wasn't sealed, so I sneaked a peek. She had signed it

Rebecca but had also added a bunch of *xoxoxoxo*'s below her name.

We were definitely doing the right thing.

I got busy in the kitchen, whisking eggs and milk and adding a bit of cinnamon to make Mom's famous French toast. I took some bacon out of the fridge and dumped the whole pack into a pan. I knew Rory wanted some for his wrap today, plus Dad was a sucker for bacon with his French toast. The smell and sizzle must have traveled up the stairs. Rory soon stumbled into the kitchen, wearing Batman boxers and a ratty T-shirt full of holes.

"Why didn't you wake me?" he asked, running his hand through his hair.

"I just got things started," I said.

"So about that website thing," Rory said. "I don't think we should do it.

It's kind of a lame gift. I was thinking about it a lot last night when I couldn't sleep."

I pointed to the card Rebecca had left. "She signed it *x's and o's*."

"How do you know?" Rory asked.

"Bacon is almost ready," I said, ignoring him. "I made extra for your lunch."

"Did you look at the card?"

"You need to help get breakfast ready too, okay? We always do this together."

"Okay, okay. I'll make the coffee," said Rory. "But you shouldn't look at other people's cards, you know."

"Whatever," I said. "Hurry up with that coffee, will you? Dad is going to be up soon. Maybe you could let Curly out too."

"I already did," said Rory. "I took her out front. Jeez, you're bossy this morning."

"Whatever," I snapped.

I was so busy flipping the French toast and putting bacon on paper towels that I didn't hear Dad come in.

"Wow! Smells amazing in here," he said.

I turned away from the stove and smiled at him. "Mom's recipe," I said. "Happy birthday! You deserve someone who can cook for you like Mom used to."

He ran his hand through his hair just like Rory had, but his was seriously sticking up all over the place. "I'm impressed," he said.

"Sit down, Dad," said Rory. "I'm your bar-i-sta this morning." He tried to speak with an Italian accent and made big gestures with his hands.

Dad laughed. He always laughs at Rory and his lame jokes. Then he sat down in the same spot he sits every morning. Rory handed him his coffee and the newspaper. My dad is a bit old-fashioned and still likes to read a real newspaper every morning. He picked up the card from Rebecca and opened it. When I heard him laugh again, I turned back to the stove. I couldn't watch. Or listen.

"Do you want to open your presents before or after breakfast?" Rory asked.

"Well, breakfast is ready now, so why don't we eat first?" I said before Dad could answer.

"Just need to add the finishing touches…" said Rory. He sprayed the whipped cream on the French toast and placed the strawberries on top. One by one, he carried the plates to the table.

"Just like your mother's," said my dad, looking at his plate.

Suddenly a weird silence filled the room. I quickly sat down and picked up the plate of bacon. I passed it to my father.

"This sure is a treat," he said. His voice was a bit flat now.

We all ate without speaking for the next few minutes. Forks scraping on plates was the only sound. Well, except for the odd whine from Curly, hoping for bacon scraps. Finally Dad asked us a few questions about work. I let Rory answer. I kept watching Dad, waiting for the perfect time.

He was just taking his last bite when I said, "Rory, let's give Dad his gifts."

"I don't need gifts," said Dad. 'You know that."

"Cards then," I said.

"And one gift." Rory handed him the gift bag he'd had stashed under his chair.

Even though Dad still grumbled a bit that we didn't need to get him anything, he opened the bag and pulled out the shirt. I wanted to groan because it really was ugly. But Dad's face lit up like a firecracker. "I love it!" he said.

"I knew you would," said Rory.

Dad gave Rory a hug first and then he hugged me.

"We still have our cards and one more little gift," I said. "But it's not something we bought, so don't worry."

"Homemade gifts are the best," he said.

"Cards first," said Rory.

We both handed him our cards and watched him open them up. He always cries when he reads our words. He took off his glasses and wiped his eyes. Then he put his glasses back on and looked at us. "Thank you so much, both of you," he said, his voice cracking a little. "I'm so lucky to be your dad."

More hugs. Longer hugs. Birthdays always got this way, ever since Mom died.

"O-kay," I said. My voice was a little higher than normal. Was I nervous? Actually, I guess I was. What if he was offended by the idea? "Last gift,"

I managed to squeak out. No turning back now.

"I don't need anything more," he said. "Honestly. The cards are enough. You've made an old man happy."

I looked at Rory, but he was picking at his nails, head down.

"It didn't cost us anything, Dad. And you're not old." I sucked in a deep breath and then just blurted it out. "Rory and I want to set you up on this site called *Organic Love dot com*! We think it sounds perfect for an eligible bachelor like you."

Rory looked up at me quickly. "It…it wasn't really my idea," he said.

I could have punched him. *Sure, throw me under the bus*. Dad looked completely confused. He frowned and pressed his fingers to his temples.

"Um," said Dad. "Organic what?"

"Organic Love dot com," I said.

"It's a website?"

I was prepared. I logged in to my laptop and quickly pulled up the website. I turned the screen toward my father. He was still frowning as he looked at it. I held my breath, waiting for him to say something, anything.

"Is this…for dating or for ordering food?"

"Dating!" I said way too high and loud. "Rory and I will build a profile for you for your birthday. That's our gift. See? No money. It's free."

"But…I'd have to go on a date? Do we go out for organic food or something?"

"No, no. The name has nothing to do with food. You just go out on a regular date," I said.

"Oh." He leaned back in his chair. He ran his hand through his messy hair again. "I'm not sure I'm ready for this."

I kind of knew he was going to say that, so I had an answer ready. "What about going on three dates, to see how you feel. That's all. And if they don't work out, then so be it."

"Three?"

"Just three," I said, nodding. "All you have to do is meet for coffee on the first date."

"How do you even know about this?" he asked.

"A guy at the camp told us about it," said Rory. "His dad uses this site. He said the first date is always just for coffee."

"Are you two…worried about me?" my dad said, still frowning.

I kissed him on the cheek. "No! But we want you to be happy, Dad."

"But I *am* happy. I have you two, and Rebecca is here helping. It's all good."

"*Pleeeeeease*," I said.

Dad blew out a big breath of air. "Okay, so just coffee?"

"That's it. That's all. And if you two

hit it off and you find her smart, like you can talk to her about science and stuff, then maybe you'll want to go on another date, and then who knows?"

This time when my dad exhaled he sounded like a horse. "You really want me to do this?"

I wrapped my arms around his neck. "I knew you'd say yes, Dad."

He patted my back. "Just three," he muttered.

Chapter Five

"What are we going to say?" Rory stared at the computer screen. "What *are* Dad's hobbies?"

We'd rushed home right after camp to finish filling in Dad's profile. "We have to think about this," I said. "Let's start with his job. I did mention science to Dad."

"Yup, he's a biology professor all right," said Rory. "So that means he likes biology. Put that down."

"It's not exactly exciting," I said.

"Yeah, but it's him. He reads that *Science and Cell* magazine from cover to cover every month."

"Okay," I said. I typed *biology* in one of the hobby slots. "We need three. Let's think of something not work related."

"He likes to ride his bike," said Rory.

My dad has one of those old-fashioned bikes with a basket up front and a rat trap in the back. A *rat trap*—that's what he called it. Seriously. It's some olden-day thing. He likes to ride to the grocery store. I told him he had to get a basket because the bread was always getting squished in the rat trap. He also rides his bike to work when he doesn't have to drive us anywhere.

"Yeah. Okay," I said. I typed in *bike riding*. "Okay, I need one more."

Both of us sat there thinking. Finally Rory flopped back on my bed. "This is too hard."

"I've got it!" I yelled. "*Chess*."

Rory sat right up. "That's a good one! The best yet."

"Okay, so now we need a photo," I said. "We need to make him look cool."

"Right," said Rory. "And that's not easy."

"Well, let's just hope that when he gets a date, he doesn't wear that shirt you gave him. Come on. Let's go downstairs."

As soon as I hit the bottom step, I heard my dad and Rebecca laughing. I'd thought she was done for the day. I walked into the kitchen. Dad was leaning all casual like against the counter. Rebecca looked like a storm had taken her by surprise. Her hair was a frizzy mess.

"Um," I said. "Dad, could we see you for a second?"

He glanced over at us. "Sure. What's going on?"

Rebecca glanced at the kitchen clock. "I should get going. I have to pick up my kids."

Rebecca has two kids, Cassie and Lance. Cassie is ten and Lance has just turned eight. In the summer they usually come to work with her, but sometimes she puts them in day camps. Dad has always insisted that her kids are welcome at our place anytime. Most of the time it's been fine, but sometimes Cassie goes through my things or plays in my room without asking. *That* is not fine.

Rebecca picked up her purse.

"See you tomorrow," said my dad.

"Yeah, see you," I said.

Once she was gone, I held up my phone. "Dad," I said. "We need to snap a good picture of you for the site."

"Oh, okay," he said, but he didn't move away from the counter. "You're still serious about this organic thing?"

"Let's take it outside," I said. "Maybe by the barbecue?"

"So I look manly." My dad grinned and puffed up his chest. Of course, Rory thought this was really funny too.

"Yeah, we could have you leaning against it, looking all cool," said Rory. "Maybe even wearing a cowboy hat." He pretended to lift a hat off his head. "Howdy, partner."

Dad and Rory started a little comedy routine.

"Yeah, and I could put a toothpick between my teeth," said Dad.

"Come on," I said, a bit impatiently. "Let's get this done. No cowboy boots. No toothpicks."

"Yes, ma'am," said Rory.

I gave him my best evil eye, but it was kind of hard because he was being a little funny. Then I laughed because I couldn't keep it in anymore. "You guys are nuts," I said. I pushed them both outside and got Dad to stand by the railing, with his arms crossed casually.

"You look good, Dad." I held up my phone and took the photo.

"Let me see," said Rory.

I turned my phone so he could see. Dad came over and looked too. "I think I look too serious," he said.

"Okay, we'll take another one. Maybe one with you holding Curly," I said.

"Yeah!" said Rory. "You sure get lots of attention from the ladies when you walk Curly in the park." Dad looked a bit embarrassed when Rory said this.

We spent another few minutes taking photos, some with Curly, some without.

Then I said, "I think we have enough. I like the one where you look super casual best. And this one with Curly."

"Me too," said Dad. But then he exhaled. "But I'm still not sure about this."

"It will be fine," said Rory, patting his shoulder. "Maybe you'll meet some hot chick who digs dogs."

"Seriously, Rory," I said, rolling my eyes. "Okay, come inside and help me post this."

Dad didn't join us. Instead he started prepping to get some hot dogs going on the barbecue. He can't cook very well, but he does okay on the grill. Rory and I sat at the kitchen table and uploaded Dad's photo on his laptop.

It didn't take long. "Okay, we're all set," I said. Then I sat back and looked at my dad, smiling out at me from the computer.

Suddenly the laptop pinged. I leaned forward. "Dad!!" I yelled.

He came running into the house, the screen door slamming. "What's wrong?"

I pointed to the laptop. "You got a hit."

"It's called a *match*." Rory used Trevor's quotation marks.

"Okay, okay," I said. "*Match*. I get it. This is so exciting!"

Dad frowned. I clicked on the link, and we all stared at the woman's photo. It looked like she was working in some sort of lab.

"Look, Dad. She loves biology," I said. "And she has a dog!" I reached down and patted Curly. "You worked."

"We nailed it!" Rory actually sounded excited. He held up his hand for a high five.

"Uh-oh," said Dad. "I left the hot dogs on the barbecue."

I turned around, looked outside and saw the smoke swirling.

Chapter Six

On the day of my dad's first coffee date, I kept sneaking to the corner of the art room to look at my phone. Every time there was no text from my dad, I sighed in relief. His date was at three o'clock, and I didn't want him to bail. After around the tenth time, Belinda came up to me and whispered, "Put your phone away."

I nodded. "Sorry. I'm just worried about something."

"It will be lunch soon. You can check whatever it is then."

"Okay." I shoved my phone into my back pocket and went back to the craft table to help Abigail with her yarn monster.

At lunch we all gathered at our table, and once again I was across from Victor and beside Trevor. It was as if we all just gravitated to the same old, same old. It made me think about my dad. Was he going to just gravitate back to Rebecca? If today's coffee was a bust, he only had to go on two more dates.

"What's the matter with you?" Trevor asked.

"Just thinking about something." I bit into the turkey sandwich I had made. It should have tasted good, but my mouth had this metallic taste. I was that nervous.

"She's worried about my dad and his *match* today," said Rory.

"You got him set up!" Trevor held up his hand for a high five.

With little enthusiasm and a red face, I slapped. I didn't really want *everyone* knowing our business. But that was Rory—just blab it all out.

"You should have seen the computer program one of the kids set up today," said Victor. He smiled at me. I knew what he was doing...changing the subject.

"It was all about flatulence." He laughed. "And he even made the noises on the computer. It was actually quite genius." I looked at Victor's almost serious face. Suddenly I laughed too. And it felt good.

"Flatulence?" Charlotte asked. "I don't think I know that word." I had been amazed by how fast Charlotte learned English after moving to Canada.

But she still found words she'd never heard of once in a while.

"It's farts," said Trevor. Then he lifted his leg and pretended to fart.

"Gross!" I said.

"Well, that's what flatulence is! Victor just wants to use big words."

"Maybe he just wants to use proper words." Why was I defending him?

"So is the program really about gas?" Charlotte asked. "That's really funny."

"We had to label it *passing gas*," said Victor. "But the kids were all giggling and whispering behind their hands." He shrugged. "Fart jokes are funny. My dad still tells them. They never get old."

We all laughed. It was true.

Then Trevor pretended to let another one go.

Rory howled and copied Trevor. Okay, it was time for me to leave. I got up from the table. "Back to work," I said.

"I'll walk with you," said Victor.

"Sure," I said, smiling at him.

As soon as the day was over, I packed up my stuff. "Come on, Rory, we have to get home."

"What's the hurry?" Rory asked.

"It's four o'clock. Dad had his coffee date at three."

"But Trevor was going to come over and wants me to wait for him," said Rory.

"Okay, well, you walk with him," I said. "I'm leaving now. I want to find out how Dad's date went."

"See you at home then," he said.

Once I was out on the street, I ran all the way home. When I got to our house I was shocked to see Dad outside playing soccer with Rebecca and her kids. Lance had the ball and was running toward Dad.

"You're not going to get by me," said Dad. Of course, he did a big fake move, and Lance raced by him. Cassie jumped up and down. Dad laughed. I didn't get why. It wasn't *that* funny.

I was concerned that Dad was home already. Not a good sign. His date must have been a bust.

"You can be on my team, Jillian!" Cassie called out.

As much as I wanted to pull Dad aside, it was hard to ignore Cassie jumping up and down and waving at me. "Come on, Jillian. Be on my team. *Please*."

I couldn't say no, even though I desperately wanted to talk to Dad. I dropped my backpack and ran over to her. Cassie is a great little soccer player, and we often go to her games.

Cassie cupped her hands around her mouth. "Girls against boys! We're going to kick some butt." She glanced over at

Rebecca. "Come on, Mom. You're on our team."

Rebecca smiled and ran over to us.

I slapped hands with Cassie and Rebecca. Cassie got the soccer ball and kicked it toward Rebecca. But she missed. My dad stopped it and passed it over to Lance. Rebecca ran forward, looking a bit like a duck, and tried to intercept. She missed again.

"*Moooom,*" complained Cassie. "You just let him have it."

We horsed around for a while, not really playing a game. Then Rory and Trevor showed up. They joined in too, and when Trevor got the ball he did some fancy moves. Cassie got super excited. She whispered, "He's good."

"Yeah," I said. "He plays on the A team. He lives and breathes sports."

"Wow." Then she cupped her hands around her mouth again. "Trevor! You're on our team. Mom's not playing anymore."

I hadn't noticed that Rebecca was heading into the house. My dad was watching her too.

"I'm done too," he said. "You kids keep playing though."

Uh-oh. This wasn't good. "Dad!" I called out. "I need to talk to you about something." I turned back to Cassie. "I have to talk to my dad for a second."

Then I turned to Trevor. "Maybe you can teach Cassie that cool trick you just did."

"Sure," said Trevor, puffing up a bit. I tried not to roll my eyes.

I ran over to Dad, who had stopped to wait for me. I walked with him toward the house.

"What's up?" Dad asked.

What's up? Was his date that forgettable? "Um, I was just wondering… how was coffee?" I sort of whispered. "Did you meet Darby?"

"Yeah, I did. She seemed nice. She invited me to her farm tomorrow. I said only if we could all go, because I like to spend Saturday with my kids. She thought that was a great idea. What do you think?"

I swear my eyes bugged out of my head. A second date! My dad had a second date! There were so many questions I wanted to ask. But since it was looking like I was going to meet her in person in less than twenty-four hours, I figured they could wait.

Chapter Seven

"What kind of farm are we going to?" Rory stood at the door of my bedroom, wearing his standard shorts, flip-flops and an old T-shirt.

"I'm not sure, but flip-flops are probably not the best shoes."

"Why, are we slopping through poop?"

"I hope not," I said.

"I'm going to ask Dad." Rory left, and I went to my closet and rifled through my clothes. A farm meant jeans. But what about jean shorts? Sneakers, for the closed toes. And a tank top because it was summer. But maybe I'd take a thin jacket too, just in case.

When I got downstairs I saw that Dad had made oatmeal and toast. He was sitting at the table with his newspaper and coffee.

"This should be fun." I said, sitting down beside him.

Dad glanced at me and in his chipper morning voice said, "Yes. And it's a beautiful day outside."

"What kind of animals are on this farm?" I spread some jam on my toast.

"I'm not sure. But, apparently, Darby loves all animals. That's what she told me yesterday anyway."

"Her photo looked nice." I took a bite.

"Oh," he said. "Yes, it was a nice photo. I guess she was pleasant enough."

We finished breakfast, then piled into the car. I *let* Rory ride shotgun because I wanted the day to start off right, with everyone in a good mood. The farm was about half an hour away, according to my map app. My dad drove like he always does—slow, with one arm out the window. He had the radio on some oldies station and knew the words to every song they played. I sat back and stared out the window, listening to him sing. It was nice. We left the city behind us and soon were driving along fields spotted with horses and the odd donkey. And some cows.

I was hoping Darby had horses. Horses would be so cool. I'd studied her profile again the night before. She looked really pretty. Her hair was shiny, and her outfit looked classy. But there weren't any details or pictures of her farm.

It just said she owned a "hobby farm." I wasn't sure what that was, exactly, but it sounded amazing. I guess I could have asked Dad more questions, but it seemed enough that we were going to meet her.

After a while my phone announced, "In five hundred yards, turn left."

We made that turn and a few more. Soon we were bumping along a dirt road full of potholes.

"Holy," said Rory. "She lives in the boonies."

"Maybe we'll get to ride horses," I said. "That would be fun."

The road ended, and we pulled into what looked like a junkyard. I'm not kidding. In the driveway an old rusty tractor sat beside an even older car with no windshield. A fence that needed painting surrounded a yard with a lawn that looked like only part of it had been mowed. I spotted a goat munching away on the grass. Okay, so she had goats.

They must eat the grass. The house was also a peeling disaster, with windows that were smeared with grime. Had the goat licked them?

"Oh wow," said Rory. "I *definitely* wore the wrong shoes."

"The house does need a little work," said my dad.

Suddenly the front door of the house swung open and a woman walked out. She was wearing knee-high rubber boots caked in mud, big baggy pants and a long denim shirt. Behind her a Saint Bernard bounded out.

"Is…that Darby?" I asked.

"Yes, that's her," said my dad.

"Okay…" I said under my breath. My dad got out of the car, so I did too.

"Hello!" she called out to us as we walked over. Rory's flip-flops squeaked and slid. I grabbed his arm.

"I thought you were going to change your shoes," I whispered in his ear.

"Yeah, well, I didn't," Rory whispered back. "I don't see any horses. But she has a dog."

"Darby," said my father when we got close enough for me to really look at her. Her hair was pulled into a messy ponytail. It sure didn't look like it had in her photo. "I'd like you to meet my kids. Rory and Jillian."

Right then the dog jumped on me, and I almost fell over. I like dogs, but this one was *huge*. And it smelled so bad.

"Cocoa, down," she said. "Sorry, he probably stinks. He just rolled in some cow dung in the neighbor's yard. It's his favorite thing to do."

I tried to smile. But my hands were now covered in manure. And so were my bare legs.

"Twins, eh?" said Darby. Then she spit something to the ground. I tried not to look down, but I did anyway, more to hide my horrified reaction. I saw the sunflower seed. Okay, we used to spit those out too when Rory played baseball. "We had some twins in my family," she added.

Cocoa continued to rub against me. I wanted to pet him, but he was a filthy mess. I put my hand carefully on the top of his head. He *was* cute. But I couldn't believe Darby had let him in the house like this! Mom would have freaked.

"Do you have any horses?" Rory asked.

"No," said Darby. Then she grinned. "But I do have something special for you to do today!"

"Great!" said Rory.

"Great," I said. I didn't have a good feeling about any of this.

Darby gave us each a basket and then took us down a dirt path to a…chicken coop. A chicken coop! She pushed the wire door open and waved us in.

I gasped when the smell hit me. Worse than Cocoa. Bird poop was everywhere. Feathers were floating in the air. One tickled my nose and made me sneeze. It was a loud one. The noise echoed in the small space. All the chickens started squawking from their nesting boxes, and one flew at my head. I screamed and ducked. Rory started laughing like a hyena.

"You can't scream like that," said Darby. "Noise scares them."

"It almost hit me!" I said.

"*Shh*. You have to talk softly. That's what they like."

The chicken that had tried to kill me flew back to its nesting box.

"Now I'm going to teach you how to collect eggs," Darby continued. She almost cooed.

She approached the first box and carefully slid her hand underneath the hen. She pulled her hand out again and put a smooth brown egg into my basket. "See? Just like that. Now you try."

"Won't it peck me?" I asked as quietly as I could.

"Not if you take your time. They're used to me coming in here every morning."

Rory stepped forward and said, "I'll give it a try." I could have kissed him.

I watched Rory as he slowly reached under the hen. It murmured a bit, but it didn't peck him. Rory pulled his hand back out and put the egg in his basket. He looked very pleased with himself.

"That's a farm-fresh egg," said Darby.

"I bet it's delicious," said my dad.

"Your turn." Darby looked at me.

I'd rather buy them from the store. I sucked in a deep breath and tried to do what Rory had done. But as I slid my hand under her soft feathers, the chicken lifted its scrawny neck and pecked me.

"Ow!" I yelled, pulling my hand back. I could see a red mark.

Then the thing started flapping its wings. Now it was moving toward me! Terrified, I backed up and tripped over Rory. I crashed to the wooden floor, which was covered in bird poop. Gross! I tried to stand up, but that crazy chicken was still coming at me. I covered my face. "It's going to attack me!" I tried to get away from it. It pecked at my arms. "Get it off me!"

Suddenly the chickens were flying all over the place. Screeching and flapping. I screamed again.

"Stop yelling," said Darby. "You're scaring all my girls!"

My dad yanked me to my feet and pushed me toward the door. I stumbled outside.

"You were attacked by killer chickens!" Rory said as he followed us out. "That was so cool!"

"Shut up!"

We could hear Darby in the coop, gently talking to the chickens, asking them if they were all right. If *they* were all right! What about *me*?

I looked at my arms, covered in scratches. Blood trickled from a few of the cuts. "I want to go home," I said.

"Yes, perhaps that's best," said Dad. "I'll just let Darby know we're leaving."

Chapter Eight

I jumped into the shower as soon as we got home. I scrubbed and scrubbed with soap, trying to get rid of the smell of manure and chickens. When I was done, I went downstairs. Dad had a tube of ointment out. He had me sit down so he could put some on my arms.

"I don't think I'll see Darby again," he said, dabbing at my chicken scratches.

"Probably a good idea," I said. "I don't think she's the one for you."

"Maybe we should just forget about my birthday gift. It was a nice thought though."

I stared my father in the eyes. "You always tell us not to give up if something doesn't work the first time around."

He scratched his head for a second. Then he nodded and sighed. "Yes. You're right."

His laptop pinged. He pulled it over and checked his messages. "Looks like someone else wants to go for coffee," he said.

"Oh, good," I said. "What's she like?"

He shrugged and pushed the computer in my direction. "Her name is Debra. She looks nice. Likes to ride her bike."

I looked at the photo of a woman standing by a bridge. She was wearing a T-shirt and jeans and looked casual. "Oh," I said. "Says here that she's a vet. That's kind of cool."

"What if she has a chicken farm?" my dad asked with a wink. "I know how much you love chickens."

"Very funny," I said. "But this one looks promising. You should meet her for coffee, Dad. Find out."

He nodded.

"You want me to reply for you?" I asked.

"Sure," my dad said. "But this week I can only go on Wednesday because I have all-day meetings Monday and Tuesday."

I fired off the note. She answered immediately and said Wednesday afternoon was perfect.

"It was meant to be," I said. I put my hand up for a high five, and Dad slapped it back. He didn't seem very excited. But that was okay. I had a good feeling about this one.

On Wednesday I raced home from work. Rory trailed behind me. "What's the hurry?"

"Dad had his date today!"

"I know that," he said. "But it's just coffee. Last time, he lasted all of half an hour with the chicken lady."

"Yeah, but this one might be different."

Dad's car and bike were in the driveway.

"He's home already," said Rory.

I hoped that didn't mean the date was a disaster. I took the front steps two at a time and flung the front door open. I heard Dad laughing in the kitchen with Rebecca. "He-llo!" I called.

Dad came out from the kitchen and smiled when he saw me. He looked happy. Was he happy? When Rebecca didn't follow him, I quietly said, "Soooo?"

He frowned at me.

"Your date?"

"Oh, that," he said. "She was nice. She wants to go for a bike ride on the weekend. I said yes, but only because I think you kids said you were swimming that day. If not, I can cancel."

"No, no, no." I held up my hands. "Don't cancel. We *are* going swimming, and we can walk to the pool." I smiled. "A bike ride! That's so awesome, Dad."

"Yeah. I'm looking forward to it, actually," he said. "It's been a while since I've been out on my bike. I just got it out of the garage to make sure it's ready to go."

"Did someone say bike ride?" said Rebecca as she came out of the kitchen.

Curly followed her, wagging her tail. A waft of something that didn't smell too good followed her. "Did you know that I never learned how to ride a bike?"

My dad turned and looked at her. "What? You don't know how to ride a bike?" Then he grinned. "Well, how about I teach you?"

"Are you serious?" asked Rebecca.

"Yes!" said my dad. "Why not? It's a beautiful day. Let's go out right now."

"But I just started cooking dinner," she said.

Dad looked at me. "Jillian loves to cook. I bet she can take care of it."

I *did* love to cook but not to clean up Rebecca's mess. I couldn't say no though. Plus, I needed some brownie points so Dad would go on his bike ride on Saturday. "Okay," I said. "I'll take over in the kitchen."

Taking over really meant starting from scratch. Rebecca had made some horrible casserole that tasted like sawdust. And it had hot-dog wieners in it. The gross rubbery ones.

As I was chopping up vegetables for a healthy stir-fry, I heard Rebecca laughing. I ran to the kitchen window and saw her plopped on the ground. My dad was picking up his bike. Obviously, she had fallen. He was laughing too. He held out his hand, and she took it. He pulled her up to standing. Something thudded to the bottom of my stomach.

They dropped their hands, and she wiped off her jeans. I blew out a rush of air. I'd been holding my breath. This was no good.

"You need help?" Rory asked.

I jumped and then turned to glare at him. "Don't sneak up on me like that!"

"Um…I didn't. Not really. I just walked into the kitchen. Thought you might need help. Dad's outside teaching

Rebecca how to ride a bike. She has almost figured it out."

"No she hasn't. She just fell, and he helped her up. I'm just so happy he has a date on Saturday with someone who knows how to ride a bike."

"He's got another date? Hubba, hubba."

"Maybe we should follow them," I said. "Instead of going swimming. Make sure it goes okay. We could tell him we're going swimming and then sneak back."

Rory burst out laughing. "We're not spies, Jillian. And he's an adult. It's his date, not ours."

"Okay, I guess you're right." I sighed as I passed a head of cauliflower across the kitchen island. "Here. Cut this up," I said.

Chapter Nine

The sun was shining on Saturday morning. A perfect day for the pool and a bike ride. I tried to talk to Dad about his date at breakfast, but he didn't say much.

"Trevor said he's going to do a cannonball off the high board," said Rory. He was standing at my door, holding his swim trunks in his hand.

"Good for him." I glanced at Rory. "Are you taking a towel?"

"Oh, right. Forgot about that."

I had a bag full of stuff. Extra clothes, hair products, two bathing suits. I'd already made sure I grabbed the biggest and fluffiest beach towel we owned.

"I hope Dad is okay on this bike date," I said.

"Stop worrying," said Rory. "He's a big boy. He can handle himself."

"I hope you're right."

We finished packing our things and went downstairs. When I saw Dad, I knew Rory *wasn't* right. Dad was wearing cargo shorts with huge, bulging pockets. *What was he carrying in them?* And he had on the ugly Hawaiian shirt Rory had bought for him. *And* he was wearing black socks with his sandals. When he picked up his straw hat, I thought I would gag.

"Where are you meeting Debra?" I asked. Then I pointed to the hat. "And you should wear a helmet."

"She's coming here. She said she could use the extra workout." He waved his hat in the air. "I'm putting my hat in the rat trap in case we stop at the park."

"Dad, you look like you're going on a safari!" said Rory, slapping his legs. "Not a bike ride!"

That is exactly what he did look like. Not some guy about to go on a cycling date.

"We should go," said Rory, swinging his towel over his shoulders. "Everyone will be at the pool by now."

I nodded. But my feet wouldn't move. The good feelings I'd had about this date for my father were starting to disappear.

"Earth to Jillian," said Rory. "Let's go." Rory gave me a gentle shove from behind, pushing me toward the front door.

"You kids have money for snacks?" asked Dad.

"Yeah," I croaked out.

"He'll be fine," said Rory once we were out on the sidewalk.

Just then a woman went speeding by us on a silver bike. A slick bike. An expensive bike. A racing bike. She was wearing spandex. All spandex. And was crouched over her handlebars like a real racer. I stopped walking.

"Why are you stopping?" Rory asked.

I quickly turned around. "That woman on the bike," I said. "She's stopping at our house! That's Dad's date!"

"She's got real bike shoes," said Rory. "Those clip-on ones."

Rory and I watched as Dad came out. He spoke to Debra briefly and then hopped on his bike. And when I say hopped, I mean like a little rabbit. He sat upright. That's when I noticed the streamers that Rebecca's son had put on his handlebars. Oh my god. Why hadn't Dad taken them off?

"He's screwed," said Rory. "How is he going to keep up with her?"

I watched as they rode away. She led, of course. My dad trailed behind, streamers flying in the breeze.

We made our way to the pool, barely speaking. Well, Rory tried to talk, but I shut him down.

"I hope you're not going to mope all afternoon," he said.

"I will if I want to."

"Suit yourself. I'm going to have fun. Maybe do a cannonball off the high board."

I rolled my eyes. "Whatever," I said. I couldn't shake this feeling of doom.

In the changeroom, I met up with Charlotte and Samantha. They were just getting into their suits and chatting about how much fun the afternoon was going to be. I tried to join in. But I kept thinking about my dad. I told them a little about what had happened that morning.

"You never know. Sometimes opposites attract," said Samantha. "It's a scientific logic that sometimes works with humans." She is a whiz at science, so perhaps she did know something I didn't.

"Maybe you're right," I said.

She slung her arm in mine. "Forget about it for now. Let's go have some fun."

We headed out into the sunshine. The boys had already scored a good spot on the grass. I put my towel beside Victor's and sat down. Then I lathered on the sunscreen. The boys jumped in the water right away. Samantha, Charlotte and I waited until we were super hot before getting in.

I was just sliding into the pool when Trevor threw a ball my way. I reached up, caught it and tossed it back to him. By now I was neck deep, and the water felt good. Maybe it would wash away my worries.

Trevor threw the ball to Charlotte, and she jumped up and caught it in the air.

"Good catch!" said Trevor.

The ball went around and around. Then Trevor decided to do a handstand, and the game came to an end. Victor turned toward me and splashed me a little. I splashed him back. Laughing, we got into a splashing game, back and forth. Suddenly the ball came out of nowhere and hit Victor right in the face. He put his hand to his nose and squeezed his eyes shut.

"Sorry, man!" said Trevor.

"I wasn't looking," said Victor, still holding his nose. "But I think I'll get out for a minute."

"I'll come with you," I said.

We sat on our towels. "Are you really okay?" I asked.

"Yeah, I'm fine. I was worried I was going to have a major nosebleed. But it just stung a little." He pulled out a deck of cards. "Hey, want to play a game?"

"Sure," I said.

He dealt the cards for a game of War. Soon we were slapping our cards down, howling in laughter. The rest of the gang got out of the pool.

"Time for the high board," said Trevor, shaking his head like a dog. Water went everywhere. "Cannonball-style. You coming, Victor?"

"Nah. I'm not into heights."

"You chicken?"

"No. It's just not my thing. I don't want to."

I bowed my head and smiled. Victor just said it like it was. I liked that about him.

"Okay," said Trevor. "I get it. But I'm going to. Anyone else?"

"Sure, I'll give it try," said Rory. I was pretty sure he'd get up there and change his mind.

"We'll just watch," said Victor.

Trevor, of course, did a perfect cannonball. But Rory, not so good. He sort of fell out of it halfway through and landed on his stomach.

"Ow! That must have hurt!" said Victor. We both cringed.

When Rory came over to our towels, I could see that his stomach was red all over. And although he had a huge grin on his face, it was clear he was in a lot of pain.

"I did a belly flop," he said, trying to smile.

I walked over to him and whispered. "Are you okay?"

"Yeah. Let's play some cards," he said. "I need a break."

I nodded. "I'll get you some fries, okay?"

"Thanks," he said quietly.

We all loaded up on junk food at the concession and brought it back to our towels. Once we'd finished eating, Victor started shuffling the cards. "Who's up for a game of President?"

"I love that game!" said Trevor.

"Me too," I said.

The game went on for some time. At one point I realized I was not thinking about my dad and his date or Rory or any of my other regular worries. We were all laughing and having a great time together.

When our last round ended, I glanced at my phone. No messages. But I couldn't believe that it was already four thirty. Dad might be home by now. I handed my cards back to Victor. "Thanks for bringing them," I said. "That was fun. But I think we've got to get going. I probably have to make dinner tonight."

"Didn't you say you have a housekeeper who does all the cooking?" Trevor asked.

"Well, sort of," I said. "We don't really need her anymore so she doesn't work *every* day. She won't be with us much longer."

Chapter Ten

"That was so fun," said Rory on the way home.

"Yeah," I said, not really listening. "I wonder how Dad did on his bike ride." I started to walk faster.

"Hey, slow down!" he said. "My stomach still hurts."

"It's not my fault you have to do everything Trevor does."

"Why do you like Victor more than him?" Rory kept pace beside me.

"I don't! They're both my friends," I said. "Victor makes me laugh."

"But Trevor is cooler."

I looked at Rory. "Who cares? Why are we even talking about Trevor when we should be talking about Dad?"

"Okay, okay. I actually do hope he was able to keep up with Debra."

"Should we run the rest of the way?"

"Yeah, but only because I'm starving."

We jogged home. Dad's bike was leaning against the side of the house. That was sort of weird because Dad always puts his bike away.

"Dad!" I called out as I opened the front door.

"In the family room." His voice sounded funny.

Rory and I looked at each other. Rory shrugged.

We found Dad on the sofa, stretched out and still wearing his sandals. His face was the color of a really, really ripe tomato. It was even redder than Rory's stomach had been after his diving mess-up off the high board. A wet towel was draped across Dad's forehead.

"Are you okay?" Rory asked.

Dad slowly rolled his head and looked at us through half-open eyes. "I have never been so tired in my life." His words almost sounded like gibberish. I could hardly understand him.

"Did she kick your butt?" Rory asked.

"And everything else," he said. "I won't be able to walk for a week."

"Sounds like a bad date," said Rory. "Was it worse than the chicken lady?"

"Ro-ry," I whispered.

"Almost," said Dad, laughing a little. "We did all these hills." He groaned as he sat up and wiped his face with the towel.

Rory cracked up. "Hills? You? On *that* bike?"

Dad shook his head. "I thought we were going for a nice easy ride."

"I can make dinner," I said. Rebecca usually spent the weekend with her family.

Dad shook his head. "No, let's just order in. No dishes. I'm going to be on this sofa all night."

Rory and I went upstairs to get changed out of our swim stuff. I hung up my bathing suit in the bathroom. Who knew what Rory would do with his? None of my business. But what *was* my business was making sure Dad's next date was a good one. I took out my laptop and logged in. I found a few profiles that could be matches before Rory knocked on my door.

"Come in," I said, without looking over at him.

"What are you doing?"

"Dad only agreed to go on three dates. He's just got one more. We need to get this right."

"*We*? Isn't it his decision?"

"He needs our help."

Rory frowned. "I'm going downstairs," he said. "Dad does need help ordering takeout. That's way more important."

I scrolled through another profile. And another. And another. I kept looking, searching. Finally I found one that I thought would work. I ran downstairs with my laptop. Rory and Dad were playing a game of chess.

"I found the perfect date for you, Dad," I said.

"Oh, Jillian. I'm pretty tired of this dating stuff."

Rory looked at me and did a slash-across-the-throat motion. But I didn't want to give in just yet. I sat beside Dad and opened up the laptop. "Check it out, Dad."

The woman had long dark hair, like our mother. She was dressed in skinny jeans and a white blouse. And her feet were bare—that was something our mother would have done for a photo. Beside her was a chessboard.

"She looks nice," said Dad.

I pointed to the chessboard. "Yes! And she loves chess!"

Dad ran his hand through his hair and sighed. "All right. I'll do one more. But Jilly, this is the last one."

I leaned into him, pressing my cheek on his shoulder. When my dad calls me Jilly, it makes me feel both happy and sad. It's what Mom used to call me. "I have a good feeling about this one," I said.

"That's what you said last time," said Rory. "Your move, Dad."

On Monday Rory and I got home from work later than usual. We'd stopped for ice cream. We could hear Dad laughing in the family room. The day before, he'd walked around like his legs were wooden poles that couldn't bend.

"Sounds like Dad has the giggles," said Rory.

Then I heard Rebecca snort.

"I wonder what's so funny," he added. I rolled my eyes.

Instead of going upstairs, I dropped my backpack on the floor and went straight to the family room. Dad and Rebecca were playing chess. Chess! I'd never seen them play chess before. Curly sat on Rebecca's lap. She perked up when she saw us and jumped off to run over to me.

"This is such a hard game." Rebecca said, laughing as she moved one of her pawns.

"That's a good move!" My dad nodded at her and pointed to the chessboard.

Rebecca looked over at me and smiled. "Your dad is just being kind. I haven't been making such good moves," she said.

"You're learning," said Dad. "It takes time to figure it out." He started explaining why the move she'd made was a good one.

I had to wait until he finished talking. (He went on and on.) When he was finally done I said, "The woman you're meeting for coffee belongs to a *chess club*. She must be super smart." Rebecca and my dad both looked at me. Dad had a funny look on his face. In that moment, I regretted my words. It was like they both knew I had said it to make Rebecca feel bad. Which was true. But now I sort of felt bad. But still. It was the truth.

"Rebecca is just learning," said my dad gently.

Rebecca laughed. "You have to start somewhere!" Then she stood up. "But I should be on my way." She reached over and picked up a tube of ointment from the table. "Don't forget to put more of this on those sore muscles of yours."

"We can do another lesson tomorrow, if you want," said my dad. He took the tube she handed to him. "Thanks so much for bringing this over, Rebecca. I think it helped."

After she left, I went to the kitchen to make a snack. My dad came in. "Jilly," he said. "That wasn't nice, and you know it. You made it sound like Rebecca wasn't good enough or smart enough to play with me."

I lowered my head and didn't look at my dad. I couldn't. "She didn't seem to care," I said. "Anyway, it was the truth." I looked up. "You always say to speak the truth about everything."

"I do," he said. "But sometimes it's more important to be kind. Rebecca is a nice person, and we're lucky to have her."

"I know she's nice," I said. I paused for just a second before I asked, "Are you a little excited about your next coffee date?" I had to change the subject.

"We decided not to meet for coffee. We are going to meet in the park on Wednesday evening and play a game of chess instead. She wants to bring a picnic, so I'll order something for you and Rory for dinner, if that's okay. Rebecca will only be here for an hour in the morning."

"Of course it's okay! I'm so happy for you! That sounds like a perfect date for you."

"Her idea," he said. He paused for a second to push his glasses up. "This is date number three, you know."

"I know."

Three is my lucky number!

Chapter Eleven

"Anyone want to play soccer in the park tonight?" Charlotte asked us all at lunch. I'd made turkey sandwiches with cheddar cheese and lettuce for Rory and me. Since we took over making our lunches, we alternated days. If the truth be told, Rory's sandwiches were better than mine. We were in our last week of camp. Although I was looking forward to sleeping in, I was going to miss seeing everyone every day. We'd made a few plans to get together. Victor and I had even talked about going for a bike ride.

"I'm in," said Rory.

"I can get some others to join us too," said Trevor. "So we can have a real game."

"I'll come," said Victor. "I used to play soccer when I was little. My father said I had two left feet." He laughed. "Hey, anyone ever see that movie called *Best in Show*, where the guy really has two left feet? It's hilarious."

"I love that movie!" I said.

"*Best in Show*?" Trevor tilted his head. "Never heard of it."

"It's old," said Rory. "About a dog show." He rolled his eyes. "Jillian has only watched it a million times."

"Me too," said Victor. "One summer it was my go-to movie."

"Me too," I said.

"Geeks," said Rory, shaking his head.

"Look who's talking," I snapped back.

"Okay, twins, don't get started," said Samantha. "Let's talk about the game. What time should we meet?"

"Yeah, we should figure that out," I said. "Rory and I have something to do around dinnertime. Could we meet around seven?"

"What do we have to do?" Rory asked.

"Later," I said, shaking my head at him.

"Oh, right. We have to spy on Dad."

"Spy on your dad?" Trevor stared at us, suddenly interested.

"Yeah, on one of his dates," said Rory.

I gave Rory the slash-across-the-throat motion. Why did he always have to share so much?

Trevor started laughing. "That sounds stalker-ish."

"They'll be in the park," I said. "We aren't *stalking*. We're just *observing*." I stood up. "I think it's time to get back to work."

"Seven for soccer works for me," said Charlotte, zipping up her lunch container.

"Perfect," I replied.

Dad's car was out front when we got home. I was relieved to see that Rebecca's was gone. I had walked as fast as I could, and Rory had trailed behind, whining with every step. I quickly checked the garage and saw that Dad's bike was in there.

As we climbed the steps to the front door, I turned to Rory. "Don't tell Dad anything about us following him. Don't let it slip."

"I won't," he mumbled.

We entered the house. "Dad!" I called.

He came out from the kitchen. He was wearing his best shorts and a nice button-down shirt with little checks. Curly bounded beside him, wagging her tail. "Wow, you look great!" I said.

"Thanks," he said. He straightened his collar.

"Yeah, you clean up good, Dad." Rory walked over to him and gave him a playful punch. "Ready for your big date?"

"Ready as I'll ever be." He puffed out his chest. Or tried to. "Last one." He patted his chest.

I took two steps toward him and gave him a hug. "I've got a good feeling about this one, Dad. So it might not be your last."

"We'll see about that. Oh! I better get the chessboard. That was the deal we made. I will bring the board. She will bring some food."

I liked that they were already agreeing on things, sharing responsibility. So far, so good!

With his chessboard under his arm, Dad left. He took the car. This was after I had convinced him not to show up on his bike with the chessboard secured in his beloved rat trap. His future girlfriend could find out all about his rat trap on the second or third or tenth date.

Chapter Twelve

As soon as Dad had backed out of the driveway, I grabbed Rory's arm. "Come on, we have to go."

"I need to get something to eat first. I'm starving."

"Are you kidding me? Grab something quick. I'll get your bike out."

When Rory finally walked out the front door, he had a granola bar in one hand and something else in his other hand. "Rebecca left her wallet on the counter." He waved his arm in the air.

I stared at the little black wallet. Simple in design. "I'll text her and tell her," I said. "Go put it back on the counter, and then let's go."

Rebecca had texted me back by the time Rory had returned and was climbing onto his bike.

"She's got a key," I said. "She'll come by and get it while we're out."

We took off, and I pedaled as hard as I could to get to the park where Dad was meeting Alison. I already liked her because I like that name. Rory kept up and—surprise, surprise—didn't complain.

"They're probably by the picnic tables," said Rory.

"Right," I answered. "But we have to make sure they don't see us."

Rory pointed in the distance. "There he is. Still by himself."

I stared at the back of my father's head. He looked so lonely sitting there. A horrible thought occurred to me. "I hope she doesn't stand him up."

Rory spotted some bushes that would make good cover. But first we had to lock up our bikes.

After we'd snapped our locks shut, Rory and I made our way around the side of the park and over to the big clump of bushes. We were lucky that Dad had picked that table. The bushes gave us a perfect sight line.

We were completely hidden when Rory whispered, "Here she comes."

I stared at Alison. Like, really stared. Her long dark hair was pulled into a ponytail, and it swung when she walked. She was dressed in cool skinny jeans and a royal-blue T-shirt.

"She's beautiful," I whispered. "And look! She's carrying an actual picnic basket!"

"Maybe she's too classy for Dad," said Rory. "But I wonder what she brought? I'm starving."

"Shhh." I watched my father stand up and shake Alison's hand. "This is exciting!" I said. "He looks so good. I bet she packed him a fabulous meal. No takeout." I clasped my hands together and smiled as I watched what looked to me like the perfect date.

They both sat down, and Dad got out the chessboard. Alison opened up the basket and took out two wine glasses.

"Real glasses," I said.

"How can you tell from here?" Rory whispered. "Anyway, who cares? I'm more interested in what food she brought. Did I tell you I was starving?"

"We'll get some food before we go to play soccer." I didn't look at Rory.

My eyes were glued to the most perfect match.

"She's putting out cheese and crackers," said Rory. "Grapes. And that looks like some kind of cured meat. Oh, and something in a container."

"That means it's homemade. Look, they're having a toast." I watched as they clinked glasses. "She just smiled at him, and he smiled back!"

"Wow, you're really into this. Sort of like when you got up at four AM to watch that royal wedding."

"It's the beginning of love, Rory." I clapped my hands together.

"They're starting the game," said Rory.

Neither of us said anything. After staring at the board intently, Alison moved her piece first. Dad studied the board and then took his turn. They went back and forth for a few more times.

"I wish I could see the board better," said Rory. "I want to know how Dad is doing."

"Doesn't matter," I said. "It's the picnic that counts."

"Should we go?" said Rory. "Looks like Dad has this under control. A chess game sometimes goes on for a while."

I didn't really want to leave yet, but I knew Rory was right. Dad did have this totally under control. I was bursting with pride. "Five more minutes," I said. "Then we can pick up a sub from somewhere before we meet the gang for soccer."

"Music to my ears," said Rory. "Boy, Dad is really concentrating."

"Yeah. I wish he'd look at his date a little more."

Suddenly Alison stood up and started waving her arms in the air. She had this weird look on her face.

"What is she saying?" Rory asked.

"I can't tell."

Her face was all scrunched up. Her eyebrows were furrowed. Her lips were pressed together.

"She doesn't look happy," said Rory.

Then Alison leaned over and just flipped the chessboard over. With both hands. Tossed it in the air. Chess pieces flew everywhere. One even hit Dad on the top of his head. The board fell to the ground. He watched it drop.

"Uh-oh," said Rory.

"Cheater!" the woman yelled at my father.

Chapter Thirteen

"Um, I think we should go," said Rory softly. "Dad would not want us seeing this."

"Yeah," I replied. I turned away from the sight of my dad picking up his precious chess pieces. Alison had walked away in a big huff. Picnic basket and all. She had packed everything up in all of ten seconds flat and stormed off.

Dad had stared at her, stunned. Now he was moving slowly, putting one piece away at a time.

"This is all my fault," I said. "I made him do this."

"I helped," said Rory, patting me on the shoulder. "Come on. Let's go home and forget about soccer. Dad will need us."

We got on our bikes and pedaled home. We got there before Dad and went into the house. We had only been there for five minutes when both of our phones pinged. We pulled them out at exactly the same time.

"Text from Dad," said Rory first. He read it out loud.

Little change in plans. Had to go to work. Will be home later.

"I feel awful," I said. "He's gone to work to distract himself."

Rory put his arm around me. "Maybe we should go meet the gang for soccer then. Just for an hour anyway. It will be good for us to run around."

"What if Dad comes home early?" I asked.

"Well, at least he won't think we spied on him."

"We can't let him know that we saw what happened," I said.

"Agreed," said Rory.

As much as Rory likes to blab about everything, I knew he wouldn't about this.

All the way to the park, with each pedal of my bike, I thought about my dad. All I could see was the look of confusion on his face. How he'd pushed his glasses up on his nose. How his shoulders had slumped. How he'd counted all his chess pieces, making sure he hadn't lost any in the grass. I'd put him in that situation. *Mom, I'm so sorry. She looked like you, but she wasn't anything like you.*

Everyone was already kicking the ball around when we arrived. I watched Victor take a pass from Trevor. He missed it. Trevor went over to him and started showing him how to trap the ball.

Then Victor spotted us and waved. I lifted my hand and gave him a little wave. Victor said something to Trevor and then headed toward us.

"Are you okay?" he asked. Rory was already on the field. He'd run over to join Trevor right away.

"Why would you ask that?" I looked to the ground, to the toe of my sneaker. Was I that transparent?

"You just look so sad or something."

"I'm okay." I lifted my head and tried to sound chipper. "Something happened with my dad."

"He's okay, right? Nothing serious?"

I thought about that for a second. "Yeah, he's okay. Well, physically. Thanks for your concern."

"Of course," he said. He nudged me with his shoulder. "Let's try to get on the same team."

Running around kicking that ball did help my mood. Victor actually managed to score a goal, and the look on his face was priceless. Then he fell to the ground and did some crazy victory roll where he ended up kicking his shoe off and getting massive grass stains on his shorts. Everyone laughed. Me included. For the first time all evening.

Around eight thirty I told Rory we should probably head home. He agreed. When we rode up to our house, Dad's car was already in the driveway. So was Rebecca's.

"Rebecca must have come to pick up her wallet," said Rory.

Rory and I put our bikes away and went into the house through the garage door. When I entered the kitchen, I immediately heard the laughter coming

from the back deck. After what had
happened earlier, it was good to hear my
dad laughing.

"Dad doesn't sound so bad," said
Rory. "Rebecca has a way of making
him laugh."

"She does," I said. I hadn't really
thought of it that way before.

After getting a glass of water,
I headed out to the back deck. "Hiya,"
I said.

"Hey, Jilly," said my dad. "How was
soccer?" He was sitting in one of our
lounge chairs with his legs stretched
out. Curly was snuggled in beside him.
He looked totally relaxed. Rebecca was
in the other lounge chair. Two plastic
containers (obviously from the grocery
store) sat on the table between them.
One was full of vegetables and the other
had cheese and some sort of meat with
crackers. They were both sipping cans
of lemonade.

"Good," I replied. I looked over at Rebecca. "Hi, Rebecca. Did you get your wallet?"

"Yes, thank you!" She waved it in the air. "I drove the exact speed limit on the way over here so I wouldn't get stopped by the police. I left my license here."

"That's good," I said.

Dad sat up a bit and took a piece of orange cheddar cheese and placed it on a cracker. He crunched it, and little crumbs of cracker fell down onto his shirt. That's when I noticed he had changed out of his button-down and was wearing his "Rory" shirt.

"Rebecca usually drives *over* the speed limit," said my dad, laughing.

"I do not!" she said. Then she laughed. "Well, only sometimes." She motioned toward the cheese tray. "Help yourselves," she said.

"Dad got stopped for driving too slow once," piped up Rory. He reached over and grabbed a pepperoni stick. "It was so embarrassing."

Rebecca howled. "You did not!" She slapped her legs. And then she snorted. For some reason, it didn't bug me so much this time. She was always so good-natured. I couldn't imagine her ever screaming at my dad.

Chapter Fourteen

After talking to Rebecca and Dad for a few more minutes, I excused myself and went up to my room. I sat on my bed with the photo of Mom in my hands. I couldn't stop thinking about how relaxed Dad had been out on the deck. It made me realize something. Something that had been right in front of me all along. Rebecca was *nothing* like my mom, I knew that. But she was *good* for my dad. For all of us. Mom had known exactly what she was doing when she had hired her to look after us.

I heard Rory coming up the stairs. I thought he would head straight to the shower, but he knocked on my door instead.

"Come in," I said.

He opened my door but didn't enter the room at first. He just stared at me and the photo.

"I just needed to talk to her," I whispered. *Mom, I miss you so much.*

"I do that too." He walked in and sat beside me on the bed. "All the time. I swear she talks back to me." We both just sat there for a few moments, staring at her picture. It was as if she was smiling back at us, as if she could see us.

Finally Rory spoke. "Remember how she'd sing to us?"

I didn't answer because I had a huge ball of something lodged in my throat. I tried to breathe. In and out. In and out. Then, just like a light switch going on, the ball dislodged, and I broke into one of Mom's favorite tunes, "Uptown Funk." I stood up and said what she'd always said to us. "C'mon. Let's get down and funky."

Rory got up off the bed, and we started dancing. He was the *worst* dancer! But once when I'd said that out loud, my mother had said, *Dancing is for everyone. Doesn't matter what you do or how you do it. It's that you get up and move.*

As we danced, my mood lightened. Soon I was laughing, and Rory was too.

"What are you kids doing in there?" Dad stood in the doorway. We had been having so much fun, we hadn't heard him come up the stairs. He was holding Curly in his arms. Rebecca must have left.

Rory answered, "Remembering Mom."

He gave us a little smile. "She sure made everything her own. She could never do anything without adding a little something to it. We were lucky to have her as long as we did." He patted Curly on the top of her head.

I stood still. "I wish we could have had her longer," I said.

"Me too." Dad put Curly down. She immediately ran and jumped on my bed.

Dad still stood in my doorway, but now he had his hands shoved in his pockets. He started rocking back and forth on his feet. "Listen, kids, I need to talk to you about something."

"Fire away, Dad," said Rory.

He sucked in a big breath. "About this organic match thing. It's not exactly—"It's not exactly...hmm, how can I explain this to you?" He tapped his foot. "It's, um, not *organic* enough for me. Or maybe *too* organic. Or, well, I guess what I'm trying to say is that it's just not for me."

For some reason, I smiled. I had to. Only my dad would fumble his way through telling us something we already knew. "Okay, Dad," I said. "I will admit, it was a lame gift."

"Oh, Jilly, don't beat yourself up." He walked over and wrapped his arms around me. "You tried," he said. "And while I appreciate the thought, it just didn't work very well for me." He let go with one arm and pulled Rory into the hug. "And I don't feel the need to go on dates right now."

Rory stared up at him. "Understood, Dad."

"Sometimes ideas don't work," said Dad. "Think of all the things in science that don't work at the beginning. Like—"

"Okay, Dad." I held up my hands, palms out. "Don't go getting all science-y on me."

He laughed. "Your mother used to say that to me too. Point taken. But seriously, a card with a handwritten message is always good enough for me."

"Come on, Dad," said Rory. "What about that awesome shirt you're wearing?"

He puffed out his chest. "I do like this shirt."

I started humming Mom's favorite song again. "Let's dance," I said. "Mom-style."

We all started dancing. Dad looked like an octopus trying to get out of a hot frying pan. But it didn't matter. He was smiling and happy. That's what mattered.

Acknowledgments

Ideas often come out of nowhere. Thanks to Jenn Plamondon, from the Young Alberta Book Society, for saying, "My dad dated a woman with chickens. They were mean." I had stopped by the office, and I'm not sure how we got on the topic, but I laughed at her story and thought it would make a good scene for a book. You guessed it. That one sentence led to *Just Three*.

I'd also like to thank the Orca team! Wow, my introduction has been amazing. My edits with Tanya Trafford were seamless. The Orca Currents line is so successful because of the people at Orca who put time and energy into these important books. And the teachers and librarians who make sure these books get into the right readers' hands.

And that brings me to my last thanks. To my readers! Enjoy.

Lorna Schultz Nicholson is an award-winning author of many books for children and young adults. She has also worked as a television producer, radio host and rowing coach. Lorna lives in Edmonton with her husband and two dogs.

Titles in the Series

orca currents

For more information on all the books
in the Orca Currents series, please visit
orcabook.com.